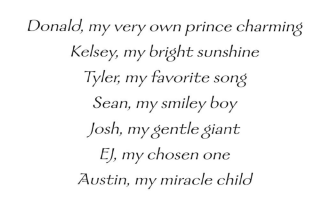

Donald, my very own prince charming

Kelsey, my bright sunshine

Tyler, my favorite song

Sean, my smiley boy

Josh, my gentle giant

EJ, my chosen one

Austin, my miracle child

And to God Almighty, who has—for now—blessed me with these.

—K.K.

To my beloved family.

—G.G.

the Princess AND THE Three Knights

WRITTEN BY

KAREN KINGSBURY

ILLUSTRATED BY

GABRIELLE GRIMARD

ZONDERkidz

ZONDERVAN.com/
AUTHORTRACKER
follow your favorite authors

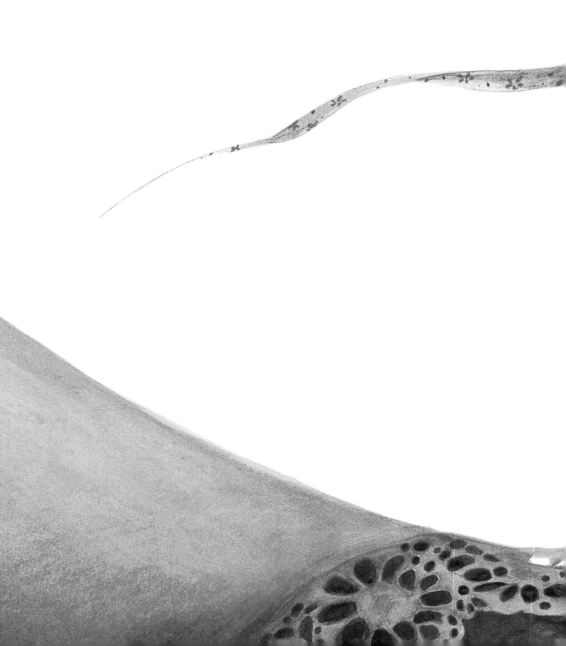

ZONDERKIDZ

The Princess and the Three Knights
Copyright © 2009 by Karen Kingsbury
Illustrations © 2009 by Gabrielle Grimard

Requests for information should be addressed to:
Zonderkidz, Grand Rapids, Michigan 49530

Library of Congress Cataloging-in-Publication Data

Kingsbury, Karen.
     The princess and the three knights / by Karen Kingsbury.
        p. cm.
   ISBN 978-0-310-71641-9 (hardcover)
  [1. Conduct of life--Fiction. 2. Contests--Fiction. 3. Knights and knighthood--Fiction. 4.
Princesses--Fiction.] I. Title.
PZ7.K6117Pri 2010
[E]--dc22
                                      2008803503

Scripture quotations are taken from the *Holy Bible, New Living Translation*, copyright © 1996.
Used by permission of Tyndale House Publishers, Inc., Wheaton, IL 60189 USA. All rights
reserved.

Any Internet addresses (websites, blogs, etc.) and telephone numbers printed in this book
are offered as a resource. They are not intended in any way to be or imply an endorsement
by Zondervan, nor does Zondervan vouch for the content of these sites and numbers for
the life of this book.

Published in association with the literary agency of Alive Communications, Inc., 7680
Goddard Street, Suite 200, Colorado Springs, CO 80920. www.alivecommunications.com

Zonderkidz is a trademark of Zondervan.

Editor: Betsy Flikkema
Art direction and design: Kris Nelson
Cover calligraphy: John Stevens

Printed in China

11 12 13 / LPC / 5 4 3

Love is patient, love is kind.

It does not envy, it does not boast, it is not proud.

It always protects, always trusts,

always hopes, always perseveres.

—1 Corinthians 13:4, 7

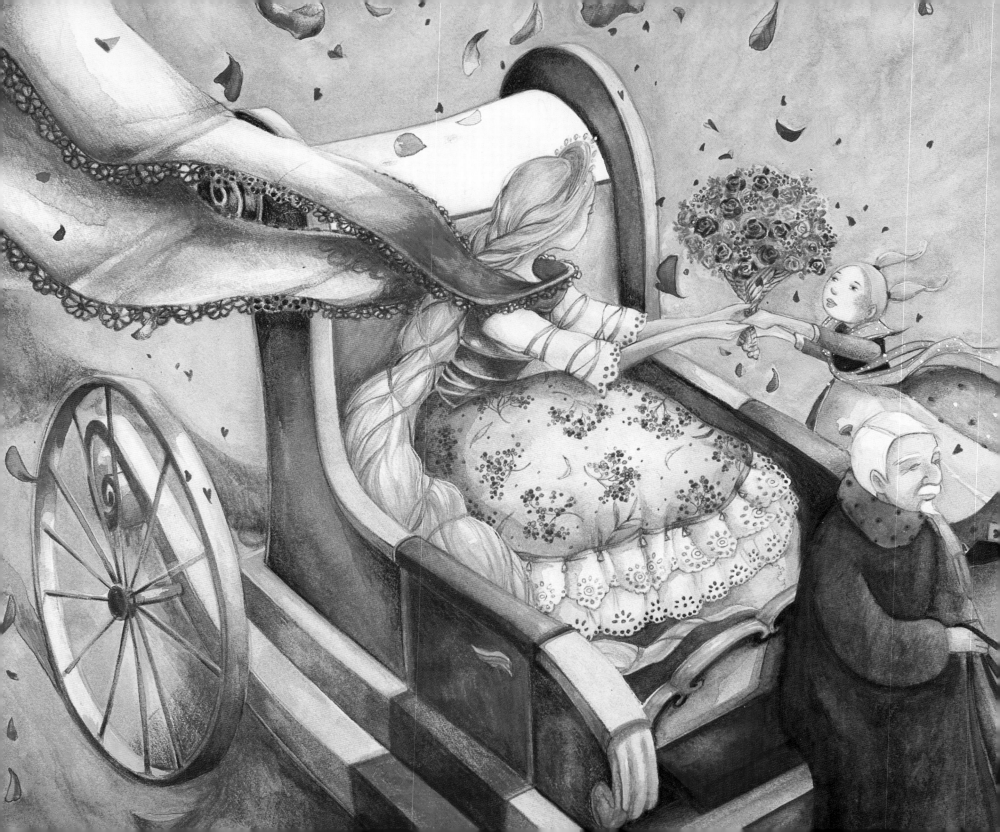

There once was a princess, the fairest one in all the land. In the busy streets and cozy houses of the village, everyone knew about the great and rare beauty of the princess. The village children waited for her to pass by, just for a chance to look into her shining eyes. For you see, as beautiful as the princess was, her greater beauty came from within.

Every eligible young knight was interested in marrying the king's daughter. Many wanted the hand of the princess because of her beauty. Others thought she could make them rich.

The king decided that only a knight who treasured the princess for who she was on the inside would be worthy of her hand in marriage.

For this reason, the king agreed to stage a competition to find the one knight with a heart as beautiful as that of his daughter.

The competition would involve tests and challenges to determine which knights possessed great courage and strength, deep loyalty and kindness, and most of all a deep faith in God.

So the games began. The knights fixed houses and ran races. They found their way through the treacherous Great Dark Forest outside the village. They lifted barrels of water and cleared fallen tree limbs from the king's field. They wrote essays on loyalty and faith.

*O*ver time, the list of potential husbands for the princess was narrowed to three worthy knights.

One knight had passed all the tests, but the king sensed that he was arrogant. Another was strong and brave, but the king felt that he was driven by greed. The last knight was loyal and kind, but the king still wasn't sure he was right for his princess.

And so the king developed a final test, the most important test of all.

The village sat on a hill near a sharp, steep cliff overlooking the sea. The king staged the final competition not far from this treacherous cliff.

In a booming voice the king announced, "This last competition is for horsemanship. You will pretend that the princess is riding with you and race your horse as fast and hard as you can straight for the drop-off. We will see which of you can take the princess closest to the cliff without going over the edge."

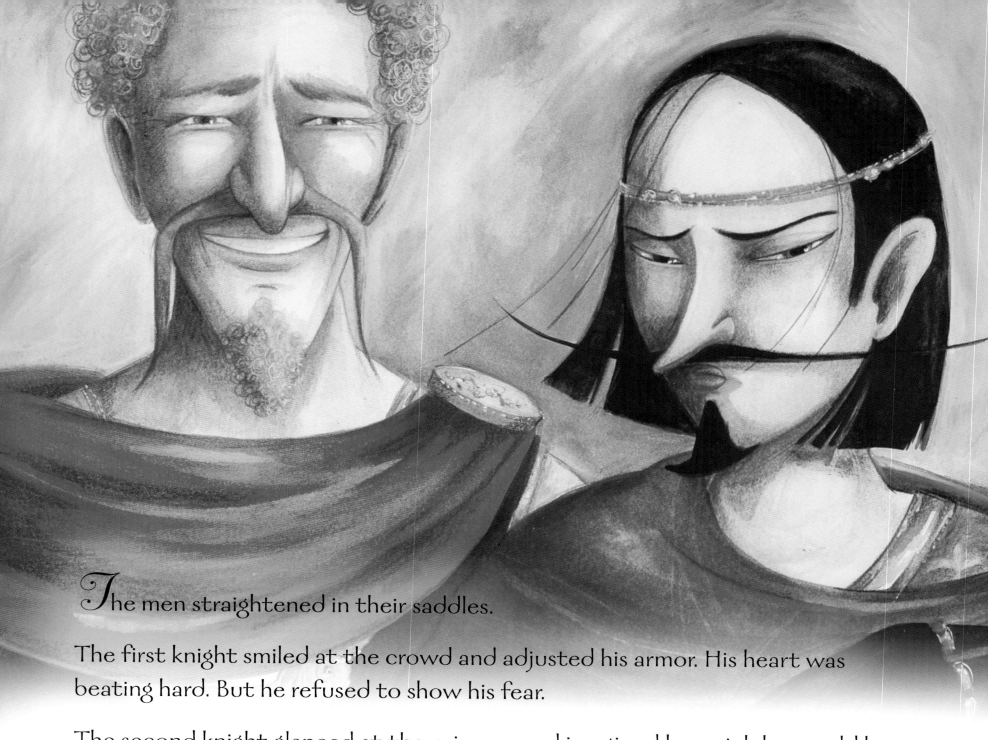

The men straightened in their saddles.

The first knight smiled at the crowd and adjusted his armor. His heart was beating hard. But he refused to show his fear.

The second knight glanced at the princess and imagined how rich he would be if only he could get his horse closest to the edge of the cliff. His hands trembled

on the reins, but greater than his fear was the possibility of more riches than he had ever dreamed of owning.

The third knight was calm, his eyes bright. In his heart he remembered words his father told him: "I can do everything through God who gives me strength." He quietly whispered these words over and over again.

The crowd grew quiet in anticipation. The first knight gave a nod to the king. "I could get the princess within a foot of the edge of that cliff."

A stirring of awe and amazement came from the village people. When the noise died down, the king raised his hand. "Very well," he announced. "Begin!"

With the wind in his face, the first knight tore across the field. The villagers held their breath as the first knight headed for the drop-off.

With a pull on his reins, the first knight stopped his horse exactly one foot from the edge of the cliff. The villagers marveled at the feat and clapped for the knight. "Surely," one of them said, "this will be the man awarded the hand of the princess!"

The second knight stared at the king, confidence blazing in his eyes. "I," he said, "can take the princess six inches from the cliff without going over."

Now the people raised their voices. "He's crazy!" one shouted. "He'll plunge to the ocean below," another screamed. But the second knight silenced them. "I can do this," he said. "I can and I will!" A hush fell over the crowd.

"Very well," the king gave the command. "Away you go!"

The stallion burst across the field.
Faster and faster the second knight flew toward
the edge of the cliff until suddenly the horse and rider
came to a grinding halt.

"Six inches!" the second knight shouted. Measurements
were taken, and, indeed, the knight had brought his
steed six inches from the edge of the cliff.

The princess stood a little closer to the king, her beautiful eyes wide and fearful.

The crowd roared for the second knight. "Who could do better?" they yelled. "The second knight is a hero!"

As the townspeople settled down, the king turned to the third knight. "So tell me, young knight, exactly how close to the cliff can you bring the princess?"

The villagers held their breath waiting for his answer.

For a long time, the third knight looked deep into the eyes of the princess. Then he turned back to the king. "Your majesty, I love the princess. She is more precious to me than anything in the kingdom." He lowered his reins. "I wouldn't take her anywhere near that cliff."

"That," the king shouted, "is the right answer! Only a knight who would protect my princess is worthy of her hand." He smiled at the young man. "And so you shall have the hand of my daughter."

The princess felt her heart take flight, for this was love. When the time came, her wedding was a grand celebration for the entire village.

Over the years, the knight protected the princess again and again. For the knight was brave and strong, loyal and kind. But most of all, his faith in God had taught him that true love always protects. He cherished the beautiful princess all the days of her life.

And they lived happily ever after.